My Teacher Is a Dinosaur

and Other Prehistoric Poems, Jokes, Riddles, & Amazing Facts

written and illustrated by

Loreen Leedy

Marshall Cavendish Children

Parasaurolophus

About 4½ billion years ago,

a new planet formed.

Prehistoric time

lasted until people started writing
things down about 5,000 years ago.
So, prehistory is a LONG time.

Please note: The dates in this book are
estimates, and facts are subject to change
as new discoveries are made.

When a scientific name is used in a poem or
sentence, the pronunciation is provided.

Plants and animals shown on the same page
are from a variety of habitats and did not
necessarily live in the same time and/or place.

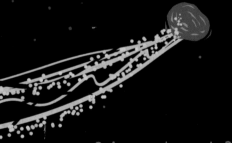

Q. Are comets popular?
A. They're often a big hit!

Q. Why are space hamburgers the best?
A. They're meteor!

Planet!
Young, unique
Glowing, spinning, changing
A world of potential:
Earth!

The brand-new planet was **hot** and was
hit by countless asteroids and comets.

After Earth cooled down, it rained
for **millions of years**,
which caused the **oceans** to form.

By 3½ billion years ago,
there was life on Earth.

The Bad Old Days

When Earth was a young planet spinning in space,
it certainly was a more dangerous place,
with hot molten lava that flowed far and wide,
and meteors falling but no place to hide.

It's good that we missed it—we could've been smashed!
The thunder was frightening, the lightning bolts flashed,
as tidal waves surged from the pull of the moon,
and rain tumbled down in an endless monsoon.

When continents slowly arose from the sea,
the landscape was rocky—as bare as could be,
without any green plants or creatures that crawl,
since Earth at that time had no life forms at all.

The breezes were toxic, the volcanoes smoked,
the air was so poisonous, we would've choked!
A billion years later (it's hard to say when),
bacteria started to make oxygen.

The life forms were simple, but slowly they grew,
then cells joined together to make something new—
since those early ages when Earth was ablaze,
life has evolved in spectacular ways!

Q. When do volcanoes sing?
A. While the la-la-la-lava erupts!

4

?

My loony celestial birth
made me a close neighbor to Earth,
though I've moved away,
and hide every day,
I've faithfully "shone" my true worth.

What am I?

!

The Moon! It used to be much closer, so its gravity created huge tides in the ocean.

Q. What do you call a rude meteor?
A. A nasteroid!

Many early Earth life forms were...

Bacteria!

Bacteria and other microbes were the only living
things on Earth for about two billion years.
Blue-green bacteria use sunlight to make food,
with oxygen as a by-product. Oxygen is the
part of the air animals need to breathe.

Over time, some single cells joined together
and slowly became plants or animals.

Q. Why did the bacteria cross the microscope?
A. To get to the other slide!

For many millions of years,
all life was underwater.

At Sea

Life began in shallow seas,
it came in strange varieties,
from algae, plankton, sponges, snails,
to squirmy worms that made long trails,

Early animals did not have a **backbone**.
They are called invertebrates. Some had a
hard outer shell, such as the trilobite.
(in-VUR-tah-brits: TRI-lo-byte)

trilobite

Anomalocaris

Q. Why are invertebrates so nice?
A. Because they don't have a
mean bone in their bodies!

Q. Which prehistoric creature
chewed its food 3 times?
A. The trilobite!

sponge

Charnia

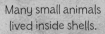

Dickinsonia had a soft body.
(dik-in-SOWN-ee-uh)

Many small animals
lived inside shells.

some had tentacles to sting,
some had legs for wandering,
the ones with shells would make a **crunch**,
when something gobbled them for lunch!

The tiny plants and animals that float
in the ocean are called plankton.

At 3 feet long, *Anomalocaris* was the
largest animal of its time.
(ah-NOM-ah-la-KAR-iss)

jellyfish

?

To win in the race to survive,
a life form must struggle and strive—
a leaf, shell, or bone
transformed into stone
reveals that it once was alive.

What rocks show the imprint
of prehistoric life?

Algae was the ancestor
of all plants.

!

Fossils!
Animals with soft bodies
such as jellyfish didn't
leave many fossils.

When scientists first saw a *Hallucigenia* fossil,
it was hard to tell which parts were its legs.
(ha-LOO-si-JEN-ee-uh)

About 500 million years ago, fish became the first vertebrates, which are animals with a backbone. (VUR-tah-brits)

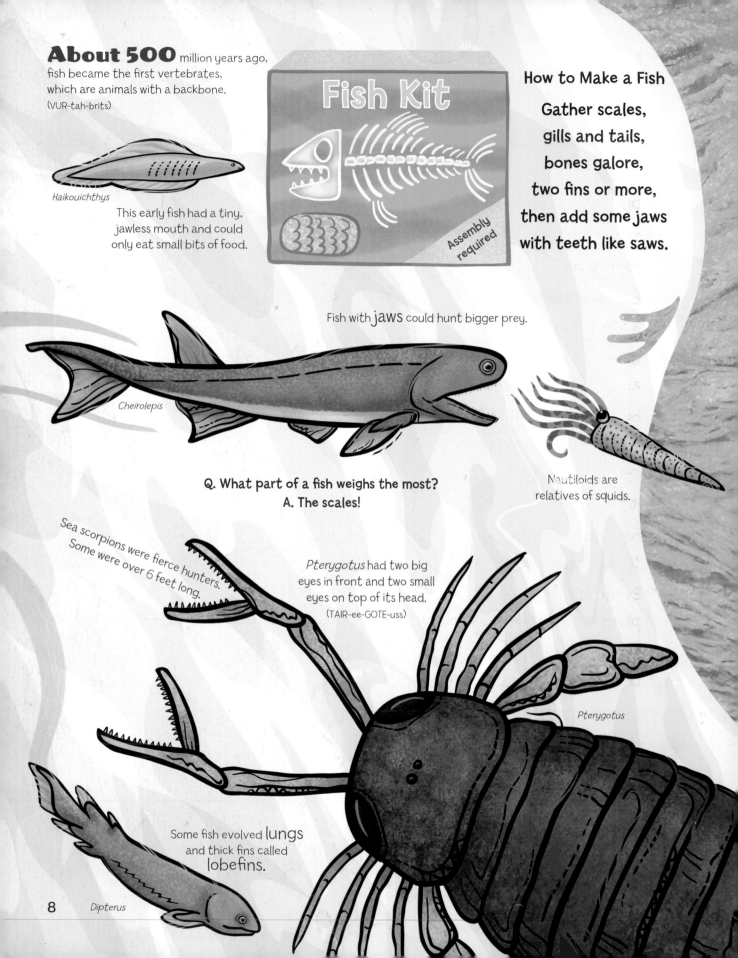

Haikouichthys

This early fish had a tiny, jawless mouth and could only eat small bits of food.

Fish Kit

Assembly required

How to Make a Fish
Gather scales,
gills and tails,
bones galore,
two fins or more,
then add some jaws
with teeth like saws.

Fish with jaws could hunt bigger prey.

Cheirolepis

Nautiloids are relatives of squids.

Q. What part of a fish weighs the most?
A. The scales!

Sea scorpions were fierce hunters. Some were over 6 feet long.

Pterygotus had two big eyes in front and two small eyes on top of its head. (TAIR-ee-GOTE-uss)

Pterygotus

Some fish evolved lungs and thick fins called lobefins.

About 450

million years ago,
plants started growing on land.

Early **land plants** were simple
and small. They slowly evolved
roots, stems, and leaves.

Plant Pioneers

They lived underwater
for millions of years,

but over the ages
a few volunteers

grew onto the bare land
and gave it a try—

by putting down roots,
they lived high and dry.

The sunshine was scorching,
it must have been rough

for thin little leaves
to be tough enough.

Eventually spreading,
plants altered the scene

by slowly beginning
to turn the world green.

Q. Do all plants need sunshine?
A. I be-LEAF so!

Lichens were pioneers, too.
A lichen is not a plant but is a
team of fungus and algae that
can grow on bare rocks.

Q. How do rocks feel about lichens?
A. They like 'em!

Palaeocharinus

Pneumodesmus

Plants gave food and shelter for small, bug-like
animals that moved onto land.

About 380 million years ago, fossils show changes in some lobefin fish.

Tiktaalik

Tiktaalik had some fish traits (fins and scales) and some amphibian traits (a neck and a flat head). (tick-TA-lick)

The Fish That Wanted Legs

Perhaps he got lost in the algae,
but one day a weird-looking fish
used strong fins to waddle as far as
a floundering fishy could wish.

He may have flopped out of the water
(despite having no proper feet),
escaping from some scary hunter
or searching for new foods to eat.

But slowly the little explorer
discovered while wriggling about,
the trouble with leaving the water—
he gradually got all dried out!

So, he went back into the water.

Q. How do you know when *Dunkleosteus* is mad at you?
A. He'll chew you out!

Dunkleosteus

Dunkleosteus was a huge, armored fish that had thick plates of bone for teeth. (DUN-klee-os-TAY-us)

Sharks have been living in the ocean for **400 million years.**

Stethocanthus

10

Amphibians evolved **legs** and **feet** that could support their weight.

Ichthyostega

Ichthyostega probably lived part-time on land and part-time in water.
(ik-thee-o-STAY-guh)

Q. Which animals are big liars?
A. Am-FIB-ians!

As more plants spread across the land, they competed for **sunlight**.

A good way to get more light was to grow **taller**. Some plants grew long, strong stems. These tree-sized plants became the first **forests**.

?

They chewed up new leaves in the spring,
a few of them had a bad sting,
each one had six legs,
they laid piles of eggs,
and some tried to go on the wing.

What were they?

!

Insects!
They were the first creatures on Earth that could fly.

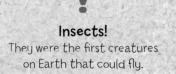

Q. Why was the insect kicked out of the forest?
A. For being a litterbug!

With a 30-inch wingspan, *Meganeura* was the largest insect that ever flew. (MEG-uh-NYOO-ruh)

Meganeura

Cocky

I'm just a little cockroach,
my family goes way back,
survival is our trademark
despite nonstop attack.

We lived with super-insects
that grew to giant size,
we knew the mega-millipedes
and two-foot dragonflies.

We crawled through changing climates
but always liked it warm;
we'd gobble almost anything
and turn into a swarm.

We've spent the eons hiding
from feet both large and small—
no matter how they stomp us,
they cannot kill us all!

Cockroaches have lived on Earth for 300 million years.

When the giant bugs were alive, oxygen levels in the air were higher than today.

Arthropleura

Arthropleura was about 6 feet long, one of the **biggest** bugs that ever lived. (AR-throe-PLUR-uh)

Some amphibians evolved into reptiles.
Reptiles could live out of water full time.

Balanerpeton

Hylonomus

Amphibians have moist skin and
lay their jelly-like eggs in water.

Reptiles have dry, scaly skin and can lay
their hard-shelled eggs on land.

Q. How are swamps like computers?
A. They both can get buggy!

?

It's such a remarkable sight,
to see a rock burning so bright—
this mineral is found
in mines underground,
with power to light up the night.

What is it?

!

Coal!
The vast forests of the
Carboniferous period were buried
and gradually turned into coal.

From 300–250 million years ago, the climate was cooler and drier.

Cotylorhynchus had a tiny head for the size of its body.
(ko-TILE-oh-RINK-us)

Reptiles on the March

Reptiles marched across the land,
left their footprints in the sand;
on the dunes they made long trails,
over plains they dragged their tails.

Reptiles slithered, reptiles crawled,
climbed in treetops, chirped and called,
shed their skins and swallowed bugs,
chewed on leaves or hunted slugs.

Reptiles marched on scaly feet
for habitat and food to eat,
digging holes to lay their eggs,
roaming far on weary legs.

Biarmosuchus

Biarmosuchus was a nimble hunter.
(bi-ARM-oh-SUE-kus)

Q. Why did some reptiles live underground?
A. They dug it!

Dicynodon

This burrowing reptile was very common.

Pareiasaurus

Turtles are the closest living relatives of *Pareiasaurus*.
(pah-RYE-uh-SAW-rus)

14

Reptiles are cold-blooded, so they bask in the sun to get warm. *Dimetrodon* used its sail to absorb the sun's rays.
(die-MET-roe-don)

Cotylorhynchus

Dimetrodon

?

As ashes fell, animals blinked,
the sunlight became indistinct,
volcanoes erupted,
the world was disrupted,
and most living things went extinct.

What happened?

!

A mass extinction!

About 250 million years ago, vast lava flows, huge releases of global warming gases, and a lack of oxygen in the ocean are thought to have been the causes of the most widespread death of land and marine animals ever known. Up to 95 percent disappeared from Earth forever.

But there were survivors...

Q. How is extinction like a road?
A. It's a dead end!

From 250–200 million years ago, during the Triassic Period, new types of animals emerged.

Famous Firsts

Once upon a long ago,
a story fossils tell,
the crocodiles began to prowl,
the turtles grew a shell,
the pterosaurs learned how to fly,
some reptiles went to sea,
the dinosaurs went on the hunt,
and mammals came to be.
The saga of these creatures is
a planetary classic,
but did you know that every one
first lived in the Triassic?

Ginkgo trees grew in the Triassic Period, and still grow today.

Early turtles **could not** pull their heads inside their shells.

Thrinaxodon

Thrinaxodon was a reptile with some **mammal-like** features such as hair.
(thrin-AX-oh-don)

Proganochelys

Terrestrisuchus

The ancestors of crocodiles were small, fast runners that lived on land.

Eozostrodon was a small, early mammal. Only a few inches long, it hunted bugs and worms. Mammals are warm-blooded, have hair, and produce milk for their young.
(EE-oh-ZOS-truh-don)

Eozostrodon

16

Pterosaurs were **flying reptiles,** not dinosaurs. (TARE-uh-sawrz)

Raeticodactylus

Q. How did the first pterosaur learn how to fly?
A. He had to wing it!

?

These animals had scaly skins, but didn't possess wings or fins, they lived on the land, some grew to be grand, and many had big toothy grins.

Which group of animals were they?

!

The dinosaurs! All dinosaurs were **land animals.**

Q. Why didn't the dinosaurs fly?
A. Flying was way over their heads!

Herrerasaurus was an early **meat-eating** dinosaur. (huh-RARE-uh-SAW-rus)

Herrerasaurus

Shonisaurus

Q. Which sea reptiles sneezed a lot?
A. The Sick-thyosaurs!

Ichthyosaurs were **reptiles** that moved into the ocean. The **paddles** of sea reptiles developed from leg, ankle, and toe bones. (IK-thee-oh-sorz)

One type of *Shonisaurus* was about 70 feet long. (SHON-eh-SAW-rus)

17

From 200-150 million years ago, during the Jurassic Period, dinosaurs began to rule the land.

Giants!

Colossal, monstrous

Lumbering, munching, growing

Ate tons of plants:

Sauropods!

The sauropods were huge plant-eaters. (SAWR-uh-pods)

The climate in the Jurassic Period was warm and moist, which promoted plant growth. The huge food supply allowed some plant-eating dinosaurs to grow bigger and bigger. And so did their predators.

How to Stay Alive

Don't be a hunter's diet—
stay hidden and be quiet.

To keep from being swallowed,
don't let yourself be followed.

Run longer, harder, faster,
and you'll avoid disaster.

To be a fiercer fighter,
become a better biter.

If normal foods are lacking,
find something new for snacking.

Disaster means—relocate!
It's time to move, you can't wait!

That's how to beat a rival
in the struggle for survival.

Camarasaurus

Q. What did *Camarasaurus* dads get on Father's Day?
A. Very long neckties!

Growing big or small, running fast or having armor, eating plants or eating meat, are a few of the many ways animals have found to survive.

Hadrocodium was a tiny mammal a little over one inch long. (HAD-ro-CODE-ee-um)

Q. Why did *Allosaurus* eat raw meat?
A. He didn't know how to cook!

Like other large dinosaur hunters, *Allosaurus* was basically a set of jaws on legs.
(AL-oh-SAW-rus)

Large Meat-eaters:
big head
heavy jaws
many sharp teeth
short, strong neck
tiny front legs
stood on two hind legs

Q. How did *Allosaurus* feel about sauropods?
A. It was love at first bite!

Giant Plant-eaters:
small head
long neck and tail
large body
stood on four legs

Small plant-eaters were ready to run away at any sign of danger.

Agilisaurus

Smaller Plant-eaters:
small head
large eyes
beak-like mouth
medium-length neck
stood on two hind legs

The Jurassic seas had giants, too.

Plesiosaur

A versatile
sea reptile.

A rubberneck
on a trek.

That tiny head
kept it fed.

Its major wish?
Lots of fish.

Its last address:
in Loch Ness?

Forget that stale
fairy tale.

The plesiosaur
is no more.

Plesiosaurs had a small
head on a long neck.
(PLEE-zee-o-sawrz)

Pliosaurs were shorter-
necked relatives of
plesiosaurs.
(PLY-oh-sawrz)

Plesiosaurs were more closely related
to lizards than to dinosaurs.

Cryptoclidus

Q. Which sea reptiles were polite?
A. The PLEASE-iosaurs!

Liopleurodon was a massive predator with a strong bite.
(LIE-oh-PLOOR-uh-don)

?

There once was a jumbo-sized fish,
too big for the world's largest dish;
while riding the tide,
it opened up wide
to gulp all the food it could wish.

What big fish was it?

!

The Leedsichthys!
One of the largest known fish,
it probably ate shrimp,
plankton, and small fish.
(leedz-IK-this)

Leedsichthys

Q. Do fishermen like to pretend?
A. They'd rather live in the reel world!

21

Spiky!
Plated, ponderous
Nibbling, chewing, burping
Not much brain power:
Stegosaurs!

Kentrosaurus

Stegosaurs used their spikes for defense.
(STEG-o-sawrz)

Brachiosaurus could
reach up to 50 feet
and was one of the
tallest dinosaurs.
(BRAK-ee-oh-SAW-rus)

Q. How can you tell when
a tree is really scared?
A. It gets petrified!

Petrified wood is
a tree that was
fossilized.

22

?

This dinosaur looked so absurd,
it didn't fit in with the herd,
with arms full of feathers,
it flapped them together
and started becoming a bird.

What was it?

!

Archaeopteryx!

It had dinosaur parts such as
teeth and a long, bony tail,
but it also had bird traits such as
feathers and a larger brain.

(AR-kee-OP-ter-iks)

Q. How did *Archaeopteryx* get the worm?
A. It was an early bird!

Archaeopteryx fossils show the imprints of
feathers, so it probably could glide or fly.
Nobody knows what color its feathers were.
But scientists think that a different feathered
dinosaur, *Sinosauropteryx*, may have had
reddish- and white-striped tail feathers.

(SYE-no-saw-ROP-te-riks)

23

145–65
million years ago is called
the Cretaceous Period.

Time Safari

Let's go to the Cretaceous
inside a time machine,
the creatures are voracious,
excitable, and mean.

Pteranodon might grab us
and fly up to its lair,
Prognathodon might nab us,
because we stopped to stare.

We'll tiptoe by the raptors
and *Spinosaurus*, too,
so they won't be our captors
and turn us into stew.

Albertosaurus munches
would really be a pain,
Styracosaurus punches
would scramble up your brain.

Watch out—he almost got you!
He's hungry for a snack!
We're going home (don't argue)
and NEVER coming back!

Pteranodon
(te-RAN-o-don)

Spinosaurus was one
of the largest meat-
eating dinosaurs.
(SPINE-o-SAW-rus)

Velociraptor probably
had feathers.
(vel-OSS-ih-RAP-tor)

Albertosaurus may
have hunted in packs.
(al -BERT-oh-SAW-rus)

Prognathodon may have
munched on shellfish.
(prog-NATH-o-don)

Styracosaurus had
sharp horns edging its frill.
(sty-RACK-o-SAW-rus)

This tiny plant bloomed under trees,
its little leaves swayed in the breeze,
with petals so small,
if it had them at all,
and pollen that made the bees sneeze.

What was it?

Q. What did the bee say
to the flower?
A. Hi, honey!

Sinodelphys is the oldest
known marsupial
(a mammal with a pouch).
(SINE-o-DELF-iss)

Q. What do you call a marsupial
that watches too much TV?
A. A pouch potato!

!

The first flower!
Once they appeared,
flowering plants
spread rapidly.

Beelzebufo was a huge frog
that was about 16 inches long.
(BEEL-zeh-BOO-foe)

?

The scientists worked 'round the clock
to dig up a huge fossil rock;
at forty feet long,
it must have been strong,
its nickname became SuperCroc.

What was it?
(Answer on next page.)

Triceratops might have munched on **magnolia trees**.
(try-SAIR-uh-tops)

Stygimoloch had many horns on its head for defense.
(STIJ-i-MOL-ock)

Q. What has 8 legs, 4 eyes, and 6 horns?
A. A *Triceratops* that sees his own reflection!

(answer from previous page) **Sarcosuchus!**
One of the **biggest** crocodiles ever, it probably hunted at the water's edge the way crocodiles do today.
(SAR-koh-SOO-kuss)

Listen, Little Mammals!

Beware the beasts
with awesome CLAWS
and jagged TEETH
inside their jaws.

A few have SPIKES
upon their backs
or slashing HORNS
to make attacks.

Or TENTACLES
to grab your throats,
or horrid HOOKS
for furry coats.

Watch out for TUSKS,
they'll make you frown,
the tails with CLUBS
will knock you down.

Such animals
are not much fun,
so if you see one
please—just RUN!

Zalambdalestes had strong back legs
and may have jumped like a gerbil.
(zuh-LAM-duh-LEST-teez)

Q. Why did the crocodle smile
at the dentist?
A. He had a filling that dentists
are delicious!

27

Did Hadrosaurs Quack?

If prehistoric hadrosaurs
QUACKED loudly like a duck,
could *Saurolophus* HONK its horn?
Did flying reptiles CLUCK?

    SQUEAKS or SQUEALS, HOOTS or HOWLS,
    WHINES or WHISTLES, YIPS or YOWLS?

If *Minmi* tumbled upside-down
and CRIED a cranky WAIL,
did *Saltasaurus* HISS in rage
when something bit its tail?

    TWEETS or TWITTERS, CLICKS or CLAPS,
    ROARS or RATTLES, YELLS or YAPS?

Would *Oviraptor* males jump up
to SCREECH a mighty SQUAWK?
Would females MUTTER to their eggs
in dino BABY TALK?

    BARKS or BELLOWS, GRUNTS or GROANS,
    SNORTS or SNARLS, MOOS or MOANS...
    we just can't tell from fossil bones!

QUACK!

Edmontosaurus

Hadrosaurs are also known as
the duck-billed dinosaurs.
(HAD-ro-sawrz)

HONK!

Saurolophus may have used
its pointy skull like a trumpet.
(SAW-row-LO-fuss)

Saurolophus

Oviraptor

Oviraptor made a
nest for her eggs.
(OH-vee-RAP-ter)

Coo...Coo...Coo

Nobody knows what sounds prehistoric
creatures made, but they probably
sounded similar to animals living today.

Q. Why did the dinosaur eat a radio?
A. He loved sound bites!

28

CLUCK!

Pterodaustro

sssss!

WAHHH!

SQUAWK!

Pterodaustro may have been pink from eating shrimp.
(ter-oh-DAW-stro)

Saltasaurus

Minmi had bony armor on its neck, back, and belly.
(MIN-mee)

Minmi

Oviraptor

Q. Why did some dinosaurs give a big roar?
A. They hated small talk!

Saltasaurus had armored skin.
(SALT-uh-SAW-rus)

29

Fliers!
Swift, fierce
Flapping, gliding, floating
Life on the wing:
Pterosaurs!

Q. What's the difference between
a pterosaur and a fly?
A. A pterosaur could fly but
a fly can't pterosaur!

Quetzalcoatlus

On the ground, *Quetzalcoatlus*
stood as tall as a giraffe.
Not only a huge pterosaur, it
was one of the largest flying
animals that ever lived.
(KET-sal-ko-AHT-lus, TER-uh-sawr)

30

Metasequoia

The Dawn Redwood was known only from fossils until living trees were found growing in China.

Bambiraptor had the biggest brain for its size of any dinosaur.
(BAM-bee-RAP-tor)

Bambiraptor

Ankylosaurs were sluggish plant-eaters with heavy armor and a tail with a club.
(ANK-uh-lo-sawrz)

Pinacosaurus

Q. Why did ankylosaurs like to play golf?
A. They already had their own clubs!

Tyrannosaurus

?

If gobbling meat was a crime,
he tried to be guilty full-time;
when chasing a critter,
he wasn't a quitter
and swallowed a few every time.

Who was he?

!

Tyrannosaurus!
One of the largest meat-eating animals that ever lived on land, *T. rex* was probably both a hunter and a scavenger.
(ti-RAN-o-SAW-rus)

My Teacher Is a Dinosaur

My teacher is a dinosaur, but I'm not sure which one—
could she be *Gallimimus*, who was always on the run?

She herds our class along each day like *Protoceratops*,
and like a *T. rex* hunting lunch, she hardly ever stops.

She might be *Andesaurus,* who could search both high and low,
she digs just like *Mononykus* for facts that we should know.

She has a *Gorgosaurus* smile that we cannot ignore—
she MUST be *Microraptor* since she wants our minds to soar.

Gallimimus was built for speed
and may have had feathers.
(GAL-ee-MY-muss)

Gallimimus

Protoceratops

Protoceratops lived in
herds for protection.
(PRO-to-SAIR-uh-tops)

Tyrannosaurus rex is
the most famous dinosaur.
(ti-RAN-o-SAW-rus REX)

Tyrannosaurus

Q. Why did *T. rex* eat the teacher?
A. He was hungry for knowledge!

32

Mononykus

Mononykus had a huge claw on each arm that it may have used to dig into termite mounds.
(mo-NON-ih-kus)

Microraptor

Microraptor had feathered arms and legs and could glide from tree to tree.
(MY-kro-RAP-tor)

Gorgosaurus

Andesaurus

The long neck of sauropods such as *Andesaurus* made it possible to reach and eat a wide variety of plants.
(AN-duh-SAW-rus)

Like the other large meat-eating dinosaurs, *Gorgosaurus* had tiny arms that seem to have been almost useless.
(GOR-go-SAW-rus)

Doodlesaurus

Doodle a dinosaur,
scribble him quick,
draw him a strawberry
ice cream to lick.

Pencil in curly hair,
plus a big hat,
lots of red spots,
and a calico cat.

Give him a mustache
and beard with a pen,
if he looks too silly,
start over again!

33

About 65 million years ago, the Age of Dinosaurs came to an end.

A Warning from the Mammals

Hey you—the one with **monster feet,** watch out, because you're obsolete!

You may be mightier than us, your size is **mega-king-size-plus.**

It's wonderful to be quite small, you hardly notice us at all.

We run around between your legs, we eat your scraps and steal your eggs.

But step aside, you **big buffoon,** we're taking charge here very soon.

The reason we're so overjoyed, is right up there— **that asteroid!**

Argentinosaurus was one of the **heaviest** land animals of all time, weighing over 200,000 pounds. (ar-jen-TEEN-o-SAW-rus)

Ukhaatherium

Mammals had remained small for 150 million years while dinosaurs ruled the land.

From 65 million years ago

until today is known as the Age of Mammals.

What caused the mass extinction 65 million years ago? An asteroid strike was the main cause, and volcanic eruptions, climate changes, and disease also may have played a role.

The dinosaurs, large sea reptiles, and pterosaurs died out, leaving room for **mammals** to take over.

On Ancient Shores

This beach is so pretty,
it's really a pity
a creature quite frightening
could jump out like lightning.

An *Ambulocetus*
has come out to greet us
on legs short and stumpy
with face looking grumpy.

We have to be wary,
his lunges are scary,
those teeth look like knives—
let's run for our lives!

In time he'll swim longer
and get even stronger,
evolving a notion
to stay in the ocean.

It's hard to conceive
but it's not make-believe,
the star of this tale
turned into a whale!

Vegavis

Vegavis was related to ducks and geese.
(veh-GAVE-iss)

Nicknamed the walking whale, *Ambulocetus* lived along shorelines.
Whale ancestors were land mammals that gradually began living in water.
(am-byoo-lo-SEE-tus)

Old News

The Prehistoric Herald
or Eocene TV
would carry all the stories
so interesting to me.
What creatures lived in those days?
How fiercely did they fight?
Which one devoured the other?
What is a coprolite?
We find the facts in spite of
the ticking of time's clock;
the stories are embedded
in layers of the rock.

Bats started to fly early
in the Age of Mammals.

Icaronycteris

Uintatherium had 6 horns,
long fangs, and ate plants.
(YOO-in-ta-THEER-ee-um)

Uintatherium

Prehistoric rabbits had
excellent hearing.

Palaeolagus

?

I never would jiggle or jostle,
a creature ferocious or docile,
concealed in the stones,
the oldest of bones,
I'm careful when I find a fossil.

Who am I?

!

A Paleontologist!
A paleontologist is a scientist
who studies ancient life.
(PAY-lee-un-TOL-uh-jist)

Darwinius fossil

Paraceratherium was the largest known **land mammal.** Related to the rhinocerous. it stood up to 18 feet tall at the shoulder. (PAR-uh-SAIR-uh-THEER-ee-um)

Q. What did *Paraceratheriums* have that no other animal had? A. Baby *Paraceratheriums!*

Primates developed grasping hands and feet useful for life in the treetops.

Darwinius

Paraceratherium

The first horses were about 2 feet tall.

Fossilized droppings are called coprolites. (KOP-ruh-lites)

Epihippus

37

?

This monster bird lived in the past,
when grabbing for prey it moved fast,
its beak was a hatchet,
few weapons could match it,
we're grateful it just didn't last.

What was it?

!

A terror bird!
These flightless hunters chased
or ambushed prey. There were
different kinds that stood
up to 10 feet tall.

Titanis

Shark!
Gigantic, toothy
Chasing, leaping, attacking
A whale-eating machine:
Megalodon!

Q. What do you get if you cross
Megalodon with a computer?
A. A megaBITE!

At about 60 feet long,
Megalodon was the largest
shark that ever lived.
(MEG-uh-lo-don)

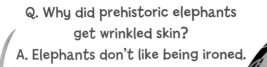

Q. Why did prehistoric elephants
get wrinkled skin?
A. Elephants don't like being ironed.

Amebelodon used its
lower tusks like a shovel
to dig up plants.
(AM-uh-BEL-uh-don)

Proconsul was related to
monkeys, apes, and humans.
(pro-CON-sul)

Proconsul

Many fossils of human relatives
have been found.

Sahelanthropus
7 million years ago

"Ardi"
Ardipithecus
6 million years ago

"Lucy"
Australopithecus
4 million years ago

39

A Tiny Question

Good
morning,
Lizzy,
you're
such a
whiz,
I'm
in a
tizzy,
so here
is a
quiz:
could
you
please
find
out
whose
tail
this
is?!?

Titanoboa was over 40 feet long and weighed over 2,000 pounds, by far the world's **largest snake** ever. It probably hunted crocodiles.
(tie-TAN-o-BOE-uh)

Titanoboa

Glyptodon was a huge, 10-foot-long relative of armadillos.
(GLIP-toe-don)

Glyptodon

crocodile

Q. What do you call a *Glyptodon* that holds on tight?
A. A GRIP-todon!

Modern **rodents**, such as mice and rats, are small. But *Josephoartigasia* weighed about one ton and probably ate fruit and plants.
(joe-ZEF-oh-art-ee-GAH-see-uh)

Rodent?

Massive, unafraid

Lumbering, browsing, chewing

Bigger than a cow

Enor**mouse!**

Josephoartigasia

Josephoartigasia skull

field mouse

Thylacosmilus looked like a saber-toothed cat but was actually a marsupial.
(THIGH-lack-o-SMILE-us)

41

Modern humans appear in the fossil record about 150,000 years ago.

Homo sapiens

?

This bulky beast covered with hair had curvy tusks ready to tear, long grass was his food, bad-tempered his mood, so Stone Age folk had to beware.

What was it?

!

A woolly mammoth!
Their long hair kept them warm during the last Ice Age.

mastodon

woolly mammoth

Mastodons were smaller than mammoths. They had died out by 11,000 years ago, along with many other large animals.

(MAS-tuh-donz)

Gant ground sloths
grew to 20 feet tall and
ate leaves and grasses.

Megatherium

Moa

Short word,
tallest bird.

Q. Why didn't the mammoth
work in the school cafeteria?
A. The hairnets weren't big enough!

Dinornis

Q. What did the tallest bird say
when it ate all the leaves?
A. I want MOA!

The moa was the
tallest bird ever,
reaching to almost
12 feet. It lived in
New Zealand until
500 years ago.
(MOE-uh)

43

diatom

Argentavis

The Nature of Life

Survival is the goal of life
from diatom to tree to whale;
each one must find a way to live,
a test that they will pass or fail.

Each creature struggles every day,
relying on a keen instinct;
all living things have just one rule:
Adapt to change or go extinct.

They seek a place to make a home,
from swamps to lakes to ocean waves;
they cling to rocks or dig in dunes,
on mountains high or down in caves.

bristlecone
pine

saguaro
cactus

Large teeth in a head 3 feet long
gave a powerful bite.

This early whale had an
extremely long body.

44

Basilosaurus

Andrewsarchus

The largest flying bird had a wingspan of over 25 feet.

Long claws were useful for digging.

Ceratogaulus

Their bodies often change with time,
they may need feathers, fur, or scales,
sharp beaks to peck or teeth to slash,
long ears or wings or claws or tails.

Each plant makes copies of itself,
each animal must reproduce;
with seeds or eggs, they multiply,
or all their stuggle is no use.

When habitats and climates change,
then life begins a fresh rebirth,
as nature endlessly presents
the most amazing show on Earth.

Saber-toothed cats stabbed prey with their huge fangs.

Smilodon

A short trunk helped to grasp leaves.

Macrauchenia

These complex antlers may have attracted female deer.

Eucladoceros

Humankind's main survival tool was intelligence.

Homo sapiens

Prehistoric Time Periods

(Source: U.S. Geological Survey. Numbers have been rounded off.)

4½ billion years ago

3½ billion years ago

2½ billion years ago

1 billion years ago

Earth is formed along with solar system

Earth cools, oceans form

No oxygen in air

First one-celled life

Blue-green bacteria turn sunlight into energy, making oxygen as a by-product

Oxygen level in air rises

Multi-cellular plants and animals

415 mya

360 mya

300 mya

250 mya

DEVONIAN

CARBONIFEROUS

PERMIAN

TRIASSIC

(continued from page 47, top)

Fish with teeth
Sharks   Lungfish
Lobefin fish
Lichens
Treelike plants in forests
Amphibians   Insects
Ferns   Plants with seeds

Mass extinction

Insects with wings
Eggs with a shell
Giant bugs
Cockroaches
Land snails
Reptiles
Conifer trees

Cooler, drier climate
Reptiles dominate land
Beetles
Cycad plants

Worst mass extinction

Reptiles with mammalian trait

Dinosaurs
Turtles
Pterosaurs
Mammals
Sea Reptiles

Mass extinction

540 mya (million years ago)

490 mya

445 mya

415 mya

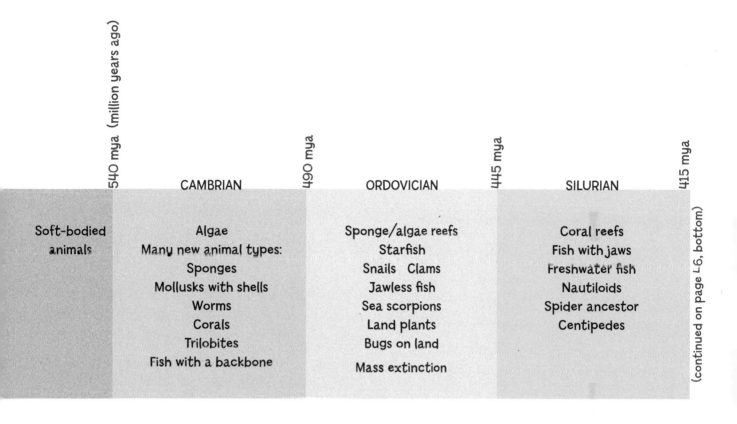

CAMBRIAN   ORDOVICIAN   SILURIAN

Soft-bodied animals

Algae
Many new animal types:
Sponges
Mollusks with shells
Worms
Corals
Trilobites
Fish with a backbone

Sponge/algae reefs
Starfish
Snails   Clams
Jawless fish
Sea scorpions
Land plants
Bugs on land

Mass extinction

Coral reefs
Fish with jaws
Freshwater fish
Nautiloids
Spider ancestor
Centipedes

(continued on page 46, bottom)

200 mya

145 mya

65 mya

2 mya

JURASSIC   CRETACEOUS   TERTIARY   QUATERNARY

Sauropod dinosaurs
Pliosaurs
Plesiosaurs
First birds
Squid ancestors
Horseshoe crab relatives
Lobsters

Flowering plants   Bees
Marsupials
Snakes
Magnolias   Palm trees
Termites   Ants

Mass extinction of
dinosaurs, giant sea reptiles,
pterosaurs

Cooler climate
Mammals and birds diversify
Primates   Anteaters
Predatory mammals
Horses   Whales
Dog family   Pigs   Cats
Monkeys   Apes
Human relatives

Ice Ages

Human ancestors

Extinction of giant birds and mammals

PRESENT

In memory of my father, who loved poetry, especially limericks

Marshall Cavendish Corporation, 99 White Plains Road, Tarrytown, NY 10591
www.marshallcavendish.us/kids

The author wishes to thank paleontologist Peter D. Ward of the University of
Washington for commenting on the text and sketches prior to publication.

Library of Congress Cataloging-in-Publication Data

Leedy, Loreen.
 My teacher is a dinosaur : and other prehistoric poems, jokes, riddles,
and amazing facts / by Loreen Leedy. — 1st ed.
    p. cm.
 ISBN 978-0-7614-5708-4
1. Geology—Miscellanea—Juvenile literature. 2. Earth
sciences—Miscellanea—Juvenile literature. I. Title.
 QE29.L44 2010
 550—dc22
 2009052901

The illustrations were digitally drawn and painted.
Book design by Loreen Leedy
Editor: Margery Cuyler

Printed in Malaysia (T)
First edition
1 3 5 6 4 2

mc Marshall Cavendish
Children

On the front jacket:
Giganotosaurus was as big or bigger
than *T. rex* but had a smaller brain
about the size of a banana.
(JYE-ga-NO-toh-SAW-rus)

At about 10 feet tall,
Gigantopithecus was the largest
ape known. (For comparison, male
gorillas are up to 6 feet tall.)
Gigantopithecus lived in Asia and
went extinct 300,000 years ago.
(jhie-gan-toe-PITH-uh-kus)

Q. What did *Gigantopithecus* eat?
A. Anything he wanted to!